AUDREY's diary

Art by Devin Taylor

Design by Lindsay Broderick

Editorial by Erin Zimring

Copyright © 2019 Disney Enterprises, Inc.

All rights reserved. Published by Disney Press, an imprint of Buena Vista Books, Inc.

No part of this book may be reproduced or transmitted in any form or by any means,

electronic or mechanical, including photocopying, recording, or by any information

storage and retrieval system, without written permission from the publisher. For

information, address Disney Press, 1200 Grand Central Avenue, Glendale, California 91201.

Printed in the United States of America

First Hardcover Edition, July 2019

5 7 9 10 8 6 4

FAC-038091-20301

Library of Congress Control Number: 2019933993

ISBN 978-1-368-04219-2

For more Disney Press fun, visit www.disneybooks.com

Visit DisneyChannel.com

SUSTAINABLE FORESTRY INITIATIVE

Certified Sourcing

www.sfiprogram.org

SFI-00993

Logo Applies to Text Stock Only

AUDREY'S diary

ADAPTED BY TINA MCLEEF

BASED ON THE FILM BY

JOSANN McGIBBON & SARA PARRIOTT

DISNEP PRESS

LOS ANGELES • NEW YORK

Hi, it's me again. This is technically my SIXTH diary since I started keeping one at Auradon Prep, and I have a feeling this will be the best one yet. So much has changed since I wrote in my last one. My whole life is different . . . better. I feel like I have so much to share.

Ben and I are dating, officially, and it's been so fun to have a boyfriend, especially one as great as him. Everyone keeps telling us how amazing we are together and what a cute couple we are, and sometimes I even wear Ben's tourney jersey on the day of his game for good luck. That's the biggest news here, but I am also getting As in every single subject this year, I was just made captain of cheer squad, and I'm even thinking of running for school council president next fall.

Things are really . . . well, __perfect.__

Okay, Ben's here—I'd better run. We have this new tradition of eating dinner every night with Chad, Lonnie, and Jane. We staked out this great table in the cafeteria, and it's really "see and be seen," all eyes on the heroes' kids, the future king and queen. __more later!__

Just a note to say I'm thinking about you, because you're the best. See you third period!

— Ben

He left this for me in my locker today ;)

It feels like I've had a crush on Ben <u>forever</u>. I can't remember a time when his smile didn't release a swarm of butterflies in my stomach, or when I didn't blush thinking about holding his hand. I still get <u>giddy</u> when I pass him in the hall or sit next to him. I love the scratchy feeling of his AP jacket on my arm when we're sitting next to each other. ♥

Growing up in Auradon, we always seemed like we were destined to be together. Audrey and Ben, Ben and Audrey. Since we were six or seven, everyone talked about us like we were already a couple. My grammy, Queen Leah, would tell me how proud she was of me for lining myself up for the throne in such a smart way. What's funny is it was never intentional—it's just that Ben and I always gravitated toward each other. You know, like magnets. There was always that pull.

Even now, I'm always sad when he leaves the room. He's the person I want to talk _first_ to when I get to school and the person I want to see last before I go back to my dorm. And yes, I definitely am excited about being queen one day, and leading the great United States of Auradon with him by my side, but for now I'm just taking it one moment at a time.

I'M SORRY, THIS IS NOT OKAY. READING THIS, IT'S SO OBVIOUS: AUDREY DECIDED SHE WAS GOING TO BE QUEEN lOOOOOOOONG BEFORE SHE AND BEN WERE EVEN SERIOUS, AND I DON'T THINK THEY EVER EVEN GOT THAT SERIOUS. HOW CAN SHE BE IN SUCH A RAGE OVER lOSING SOMETHING SHE NEVER REALLY HAD?

It's the scepter and crown . . . it's like they're turning up the volume on every bad thought she's ever had.

This year we're taking the cheer squad to the next level. I don't want to say anything negative about the last captain, but I think we were all feeling like we could be a bit more . . . challenged.

Here's what people don't understand about cheer squad: It's not just about rooting for your team, it's about generating school spirit. Making kids want to get out of their seats and start cheering, clapping, and dancing. You have to really bring good energy to the crowd and bring your happiest, most enthusiastic self. Part of that is perfecting your stunts.

This afternoon, at practice, I had everyone on the team sit in a circle and make a goal for themselves for the year if they hadn't already. One of my biggest goals this summer was mastering my back handspring and back tuck sequence. The sequence is this incredibly impressive (like jaw-droppingly impressive) gymnastics stunt where you do a roundoff, a back handspring (where you launch yourself backward on your hands), another back handspring, and then a backflip. It might sound crazy, but if you do it right, it looks effortless. Anyway, I've been working on this sequence for TWO YEARS.

That's right.

mainly I get my friends to spot me on my stunts, to make sure I don't fall sideways or make sure I get the height I need to clear my landing. I've been getting lighter spots in the past few weeks, but today was the very first time I did my sequence <u>WITH NO SPOT</u>. <u>Completely on my own</u>. I'm still not ready to do it in front of the school, but I'm getting closer.

You know what they say:
      <u>practice makes perfect</u>. ☺

CHEER SQUAD??!?
This is a joke, right? On the Isle, if you tried to tell someone you were all about "bringing good energy to a crowd," they would laugh you right off the dock I've never heard of anything so silly.

Also, what's Audrey so angry about? seeing her all vicious and power hungry made me think she must've had a pretty awful life before (and I know some kids with pretty awful lives). And she claims she has something to be angry about??

Puuuuh-leeeeease.

I've never been a huge sports fan, but every time I watch a tourney game, it gets just a little more fun and interesting. I'm serious. Ben has been playing it for years, and everyone at Auradon Prep is obsessed, but it wasn't until recently that I really started to enjoy watching it.

All that crashing into each other and pummeling each other was never my thing. I mean, I feel like that kind of stuff is very "Isle of the Lost." But then I started paying close attention, especially to the center area of the field—the kill zone. Now I'm mesmerized by it. I can't look away. Every time a player runs through, the other team fires "dragon fire" at him from a cannon, and the player has to dart around it and dodge it, trying not to get hit. It's its own kind of gymnastics, because some of the guys are really skilled at flipping and ducking out of the way.

When Ben moves through the kill zone, my heart starts pounding really fast.

Part of me is always worried something could go wrong, or he might mess up that beautiful face of his, but then once he starts running, he puts me at ease.

He becomes almost like this strange tourney ballet dancer, gracefully ducking and spinning away from the cannon fire. He flips over it and rolls under it, and he always comes out on the other side unscathed. The best part is that when he finally makes it through, he always searches the sidelines to find me. Then he gives me the cutest smile, like he

was doing it all just to impress me.
His girlfriend. His future queen.
Just thinking about him standing there,
smiling, gets those butterflies fluttering all
over again.

I heard the weirdest phrase in magical History today. Two girls were whispering behind me, and I heard them say Ben and I were the "it couple."

I don't know exactly what that means, but lately it seems like wherever we go and whatever we do, everyone is always talking about us or glancing at us to see what we're up to. We're like . . . a real-life fairy tale. All of Auradon Prep is desperate to know what will happen next—they're dying to turn the page of our story.

I first noticed it last week when we were in the library, studying for Grammar. (ICK, neither of us can stand that class.) This group of freshmen kept walking past us. They must've looped around the reading room three times, and each time they walked right past us. Then someone from the Auradon Prep newspaper wanted to interview me about the coronation—they didn't specifically mention my being Ben's girlfriend, but I kind of think that's what they were getting at. I mean, I'm used to people talking about me and looking up to me and all, just because of who my family is, but this is totally different.

It's me and Ben, Ben and me. We're really in this together.

Saving this forever. Never want to forget
this special coffee date!

CC

Culinary Cabaret

I like you, Audrey.

I like you, too.
:)

I've known Lonnie and Jane practically my whole life. Our parents have been friends since the kingdoms were united twenty years ago, and we've grown up together, playing in the fields around Charmington and going to Fairy Godmother's preschool. (She's since moved on to more mature students.) I love Jane and Lonnie, don't get me wrong, but it has always felt like I'm the true leader of our group. I'm the one who comes up with ideas for what we're doing every weekend, or what kind of outfits we should wear to the Spring Fling, or where we should sit at lunch. And I don't mind it—I really don't.

If anything, being queen bee of our little group has given me practice for when I'm the REAL queen one day. I'm good at making quick decisions and used to people following my lead.

Poor Jane. I tried to tell her not to go to EAST RIDING to get her hair cut, but she just wouldn't listen. Her mom had to run some errands in King George Town, and Jane thought it would be a good idea to go into Sir Choppington's. Don't be fooled by the name—it's a very mediocre hair salon. I mean, I really do not understand that decision. I don't. I hardly ever go to East Riding and even I've heard how meh that place is.

So apparently she gets there, and they soap up that beautiful brown hair of hers, rinse, and chop it all off. Her new bob looks like someone cut it with a blindfold on. The front is all uneven, and it really doesn't suit her face shape. There are so many spectacular hair salons in Auradon City, like madame de la Grande Bouche—where I've always gone. madame is one of Belle's most trusted hairstylists, and she was the one who outfitted her in the castle years ago, making sashes and styling her hair into that perfect French twist. She's nothing short of genius.

It's hard to imagine Lonnie and Jane ever being close with Audrey. Mainly because Jane is nice—like truly, genuinely nice. And when I met her, she was so shy she barely made eye contact when she spoke to you. (That was how it was on the Isle—no one ever made eye contact—but someone doing that on Auradon is just weird.) I guess I can see how she'd be easily pushed around by someone like Audrey, but I'm glad those days are over. She's too sweet a person to waste her time on friends who don't boost her up. (If you'd told me three years ago I'd write a sentence like that, I never would have believed you.)

And Lonnie? She's one of the fiercest people I know. She'd never been to the Isle before, but when Ben and my friends needed her help, she didn't hesitate. She jumped into battle against Uma's pirate crew, showing off the most impressive sword skills I'd ever seen. Lonnie is cool, and tough, and I can't imagine her putting up with Audrey's attitude. It makes no sense.

whatever. you got out of that battle by the skin of your pearly white Auradon teeth.

Fairy Godmothers' Day is a really big deal in our family. I don't know what my mom or Grammy would've done if Flora, Fauna, and Merryweather hadn't stepped in years ago to raise my mom. They gave her _safety_, a _solid education_, and _lots of love_ when it was _too dangerous_ for my grammy to love my mom herself. Sometimes I get a little teary just thinking about them and what it must've been like for my mom and Grammy for those first _sixteen years_, and then the _horrible_ time after my mom pricked her finger.

I was a little nervous this Fairy Godmothers' Day, because it was the first time Ben was spending time with the fairy godmothers as my boyfriend. He's met them before at different Family Days and when they've visited me on campus. And they're wonderful, and I owe so much to them, but they definitely still think of me as a child and they definitely talk a lot.

LIKE A LOT.

So we got to the cottage for tea and sandwiches, and Ben was so sweet and endearing with the three of them it made me love him even more. I really did not think that was possible. He helped Flora pick berries in the woods to use for her famous jam and even sang a few songs with Fauna. Then he sat there for about TWO HOURS listening to merryweather describe all the different things she and the fairies did with my mom those sixteen years—the field trips, and how they taught her the ABCs using different objects around the cottage. Ben smiled and nodded the whole time, and he actually seemed to really enjoy it. As we took the carriage back, I felt so happy and just . . . grateful. Grateful to have such a wonderful boyfriend in my life.

I know all the facts about what happened between my mother and Audrey's family—the invitation that never arrived in the mail, and how my mother crashed Aurora's christening and put that curse on her. It's not pretty.

Sure, I've grown up hearing the story, but it's so different thinking about how Queen Leah must've felt, or Aurora herself, or how this has haunted Audrey's family for years. The fairy godmothers must've been terrified, trying to keep Aurora safe at the cottage. . . .

Flora likes to stroll through the garden, find the most beautiful flower, and press it for me as a little present.

Things have been going so well with Ben it's easy to imagine a future together. Horseback rides through Sherwood Forest, strolls along Belle's Harbor, dancing at Cotillion, and lunching with all the biggest heroes in Auradon. (I'm really excited to spend time with Aladdin and Jasmine.) I can almost see us in the carriage to the coronation, the streets packed with screaming citizens, so thrilled that Ben will finally become king.

You look beautiful today. Just had to tell you.   —Ben

I have so many ideas for what's next. As amazing as Auradon is, there is always room for improvement. What if we had a meet and greet after the coronation so all the citizens of Auradon could come forward and tell us their concerns for our great US of A? We could even have regular visiting hours, Ben and I, to keep track of all the happenings in the kingdom. And for the biggest celebrations in Auradon, we could close off the streets and turn the entire city into one amazing festival.

Okay, maybe I'm getting ahead of myself. I can admit that. But the last few months have been some of the most exciting of my life. I feel like everything is just beginning for me.

I remember exactly where I was when I heard the news. Ben, Lonnie, Jane, Chad, and I were all sitting at the picnic tables outside the cafeteria when Ben starting talking about second chances, and what makes a hero a hero. I mean, I wasn't really sure where he was going with all of it until he mentioned the Isle. Apparently, for his first proclamation as king, he wants to . . . drumroll, please . . . bring <u>four villain kids to Auradon Prep.</u>

He wants to give them an opportunity to change. An opportunity to change!!

Can you <u>believe</u> that?!? As if these kids <u>want</u> to change, or be anything better than what they are. He said he's inviting the Evil Queen's daughter, Cruella De Vil's son, Jafar's son, and . . .

ANOTHER DRUMROLL, PLEASE . . .

maleficent's daughter, mal.

I just . . . I can't even. I tried to reason with him—we all did—but he has this silly idea that keeping all the descendants of the villains on the Isle of the Lost forever is cruel. You know what I think is CRUEL?!?! Giving a young woman a poison apple so she sleeps her life away, or cursing a princess so her parents feel the need to send her off for a bunch of fairies to raise, or using puppies to make fur coats. That's cruelty. That's wrong.

The more I think about it, the more offended I am. __Mal__. __maleficent's__ daughter. I mean, out of all the villain kids on the Isle of the Lost . . . __why her__?!?! couldn't Ben have chosen someone else, someone who doesn't have quite the history with his girlfriend's family??

I've gotten used to the idea of having some villain kids at Auradon Prep, and I am going to be polite or whatever (if my grammy taught me anything, it's that you MUST have good manners), but why mal??? why maleficent's daughter? And how is my poor mother going to feel, running into that little maleficent clone everywhere??

The other day Ben mentioned how **upset** his parents were about his new proclamation. I mean, if I were Beast or Belle, I would be, too. You spend <u>twenty years</u> working to unite all of Auradon, and then, as soon as your son comes into power, he wants to <u>undo everything</u> you did. It's not exactly an ideal situation.

I don't understand why the villain kids need to come here...
I don't... BUT... Ben told me the whole story about how he was getting fitted for his coronation suit and how he told his parents about bringing the VKs over. His dad was so furious he practically roared at him. Belle nearly fainted. Ben looked sad and confused when he told me, because he's always so determined to make his parents proud no matter what. Even though they're supporting him, they don't agree with his idea. So I just got all Ben-cheering-squad on him and told him if he truly believes this is what needs to be done, then he should go with his gut. Follow his heart and all that good stuff.

I know he needs me right now, and I want to be there for him—as his girlfriend and his __future queen__.

__UMMM__ . . . I do. I can't even imagine how stale Auradon Prep was before we arrived. All those prim and pretty princesses, and the proper princes who never stepped out of line. We've given this place so much flavor.

The Best Things Mal, Evie, Carlos, and Jay Have Brought to Auradon Prep

—__Isle Style__. Sure, I'm biased, but Evie's 4 Hearts has given Auradon fashion the extra OOMPH it always needed.

—__FUN__. Even if Carlos and Jay joke around and call me your Royal Purpleness, I don't mind. Everything doesn't have to be so serious all the time.

—__Bye-bye, perfect princes and princesses.__ Seriously—when we got here, it was like everyone was terrified about making any mistakes or saying the wrong thing, or people thinking they weren't perfect in every way. I like to believe we gave kids permission to just be themselves, warts and all. (Okay, warts are gross—but you know what I mean.)

$\mathcal{T}$oday was a joke.

Half of Auradon Prep was out front, waiting for the new villain kids to arrive. They brought out the marching band and everything. So this limo with tinted windows pulls up. Two boys tumble out of the back, fighting over something. (A scarf?? Pants?? I don't even know.) One of the kids, Carlos (apparently he's Cruella De Vil's son), has chocolate all over his mouth, like he doesn't even know what a napkin is, and the other kid, Jay (Jafar's son), actually PUNCHES Ben to say hello.

What kind of first impression is that?!?

Then Evie, the Evil Queen's daughter, walks up to me, pretending she's some sort of princess. I mean, I come from a

long line of royals, and so does Ben.
The idea that the Evil Queen is an
<u>actual queen</u>?? <u>Laughable.</u>
After everyone walked away in horror,
Ben and I gave the new kids a quick tour
of the school. I kept thinking how
useless it was, because it's really only a
matter of time before they're expelled
or just give up and go back. But Ben
keeps talking about how we have to keep
an open mind and we have to help them
as much as possible, so I'm trying my best.
Alas . . .

This afternoon it hit me. Ben's always been so optimistic about people— I mean, it's one of the reasons I love him so much. But his family's fairy tale is really specific, and if I'm being completely honest, it's not normal. When his mom met his dad, his dad was a __BEAST__. Angry, with massive paws and fangs, and he'd throw these crazy temper tantrums. If you look closely, you can still see the claw marks on the walls in the West Wing of the castle. They fell in love before the last petal on the rose fell, and that love transformed him into something better—a handsome prince. If I were Ben, the message would be clear: in even the most seemingly hopeless situations, change is possible. Love can transform anyone.

But __my__ story? My family's fairy tale? It's just a __LITTLE different__. See, when my mom was cursed by maleficent, the evil fairy, it was just because maleficent was an evil fairy. She never transformed into something better. She was always the villain of our story. There was no apology. She never expressed any regret. Instead, she's still on the Isle of the Lost, scheming and manipulating other villains. I'm sure she'd come after us again if she could.

Cruella De Vil? Still taking her anger out on puppies, probably. Jafar? Still lying. Hook? Still making people walk the plank. Ursula? Still preying on lost souls. Gaston? Still full of himself. Lady Tremaine? Still ordering people around.

Villains DON'T change. They just don't.

I tried to explain this to Ben. I really did. But he's still into this idea of second chances and seeing the best in everyone, blah blah blah. I just don't want him to be disappointed when it doesn't work out.

I turned down the hallway yesterday and almost <u>ran</u> <u>right</u> <u>into</u> <u>Mal</u>. I've been trying to keep a positive attitude (Fairy Godmother says a positive attitude is <u>EVERYTHING</u>), but I hate that she's here, in Auradon, at <u>my</u> school. I'd gotten used to this sense of safety. maybe I took it for granted. my mom and Grammy didn't have to worry about what maleficent was plotting, or if she'd strike again, and how.

my stomach hurts just thinking about it . . . there's no way mal isn't her mother's daughter. There's <u>no</u> <u>way</u> she <u>isn't</u> <u>plotting</u> <u>something</u>. You can take the girl out of the Isle of the Lost, but you can't take the Isle of the Lost out of the girl.

The thing is, Audrey's right. I was plotting something. And she's right about the Isle—I spent every second of my life on the Isle of the Lost, right up until the day we cruised out of there. It's where I learned how to read, write, thieve, plot. It's where I have my first memories. Where I made my first friends.

There will always be a piece of me that belongs on the Isle, and for the first time in a while, I'm not ashamed of that. I know who I am, and I know that I've chosen good, stepped away from that life. As hard as growing up on the Isle was, there were some great things about it, too.

Mal hasn't even been here a week and already she's ruining everything. Two days ago, in Belle's book club, Lonnie and Jane walked in with completely new hair. They both went from having chin-length, basic little bobs to long, flowy locks that make them look like they stepped out of a magazine. Their skirts were ripped, too. Some kind of strange, edgy take on a skirt slit. It's different, and I don't like it.

Then, today on the quad, I noticed three more girls with new looks. One had hair that fell halfway down her back in these perfect spiral curls. There's no way they were extensions. I made sure I stood next to the girl in the lunch line, and I overheard her saying that **MAL** was the one who'd done it. For a small price, she's been giving Auradon Prep students magical makeovers. **MAGICAL** makeovers. No one is supposed to be using magic in Auradon, especially not some recovering villain.

She's not supposed to have her spell book, and she's definitely not supposed to be charging people for different spells. It's against Auradon Prep rules, plain and simple.

Gateway magic!!
It's gateway magic!!

I tried to tell Ben what was going on with the makeovers, but he keeps saying it's harmless fun. It's like he's completely forgotten the Gateway magic seminar we took in sixth grade, where we were all warned about the dangers of experimenting with magic. Sure, right now mal is only changing people's hair, but maybe one day someone decides they'd rather have gray eyes than brown. maybe someone asks her to make them five inches taller, or they want a tiny ski-slope nose, or they decide they just **HAVE TO HAVE** flawless skin. I mean, it's <u>not ethical</u>!!!

Also, I've always believed that you should work with what you were born with. I was really lucky in the genetics department, and it doesn't take much work for me to look good, but I don't want <u>EVERYONE</u> at Auradon Prep to be able to just snap their fingers and look this way. Isn't that kind of . . . cheating???

I never understood why Auradon Prep girls are so obsessed with their looks. Who cares about makeovers and hairstyles and lip gloss and all that? I'm too busy ruling the wharf to worry if I look good doing it.

Uh, NO geNeRaliZaTioNs, PleaSe. NoT EVERY AuRadoN PReP giRl iS obSeSSed witH heR looKs.

I don't even know how to begin this entry. I feel like I'm living in a nightmare and no matter how hard I try, I can't wake myself up. The big tourney game was today, and the Knights won. Good news, right?? Not really. I was there, leading the cheer squad, and Ben grabbed the microphone as soon as the game ended. I thought he was going to give one of his pep talks or lead the crowd (there must have been two hundred kids there, seriously) in singing our fight song. He lifted up his arms and started spelling something out . . . so I lifted my arms up and started leading the crowd, too. "Give me an m!" he yelled, and then we made the m sign together. "Give me an A!" he went on, and we made an A together.

It's mortifying, thinking about how happy I was cheering with him, like we were doing this cool thing, leading the students together. I was smiling and shouting each letter like a complete fool.

M...A...L. Mal. It turned out he was spelling **MAL**'s name, because apparently he's <u>IN LOVE WITH HER.</u>

<u>WHAAAAAAT??!?!?!</u>

That's right. At some point since those awful villain kids arrived, he fell hopelessly in love with mal, **MALEFICENT'S** daughter, and decided he just had to announce that to hundreds of people at the biggest tourney game of the year. It didn't matter that we were dating, or that we've spent weeks talking and planning for the coronation together, or that he's supposed to be in love with <u>me</u>. He didn't think or worry about how horrible it would make me look, or how I'd feel finding this information out for the first time in front of hundreds of people. while he was serenading mal, I had to run over to Chad and see if he wanted to take me to the coronation. I wasn't about to let the entire school think I was just Ben's pity date.

I hung out with Chad all afternoon, pretending that I don't care and that Ben and I were on the outs anyway, but I felt like I was falling apart inside. I still do. I've cried more in the last few hours than I have in years. How could he do this to me? How can he love Mal when he barely even knows her?? Didn't I at least deserve an explanation before he went and told <u>everyone</u> he was breaking up with me???

Wow. This may sound terrible, but I guess I never really thought about Audrey as a person with feelings. Even after everything that happened at the tourney game, she acted like she didn't really care about Ben that much anyway—she was dating Chad half a second later. She made this huge deal of going to the coronation with Chad, and then it was like every time I turned around, they were together, talking over lunch or walking arm in arm down the hall. I guess I'd always assumed she was just using Ben for his title.

But "falling apart inside"? Crying more than she had in years? I shouldn't be surprised. I guess anyone would feel that way if their boyfriend (who they actually cared a lot about) broke up with them in front of the entire school. True, Ben was under my love spell and clearly wouldn't have gone about things that way normally, but Audrey didn't know that at the time. She thought he really had developed feelings for me and decided to end it right then, at the tourney game. IN FRONT OF EVERYONE.

If I'm being honest, I think I would've cried, too.

Ack! I keep replaying it <u>over</u> and <u>over</u> in my head, and every time I do, I just get angrier. You know what's <u>R-I-D-I-C-U-L-O-U-S</u>?!?! The idea that <u>MY</u> boyfriend, <u>MY Ben</u>, would choose maleficent's daughter over me. The idea that he wouldn't at least give me a heads-up first, or say that his feelings had changed, so I didn't have to find out in front of hundreds of people.

It's <u>ridiculous</u> that I have to watch them now, walking down the hall together or holding hands. It's <u>ridiculous</u> that people are actually taking Mal seriously. She's a <u>villain kid</u>, and she'll always be a villain kid. Who cares if she's dating Ben?!?!?

One of the worst parts of yesterday's tourney game was seeing Lonnie up in the stands dancing with Evie and Mal. She was laughing and smiling and looked like she was having the best time with them. All while Ben was broadcasting to Auradon Prep that he'd dumped me.

I'd always considered Lonnie MY friend, a fellow hero's kid who knows good from evil. Now I just consider her a traitor.

Family Day has always been one of my _favorite_ days at Auradon Prep. As hard as everything has been with the breakup, I kept thinking that Family Day was just around the corner and if anything could cheer me up, that would. My grammy loves coming to campus and catching up with all her friends, meeting my teachers, and visiting my dorm. Last year Flora, Fauna, and Merryweather came, too, and we had a big picnic with Ben and his parents out on the quad.

And it started out great. We heroes' kids have this tradition of singing "Be Our Guest" to the crowd at the opening of every Family Day. This year I had the idea to do the routine with these blue napkins from the dining hall, using them as a prop, and it added this cool visual element that we'd never had before. Afterward, parents kept coming up to me and telling me how impressive the routine was and complimenting me on my outfit, and when I had to tell them Ben and I weren't dating anymore, they looked shocked and confused. (I won't name names, but someone even said Ben couldn't do better than me.) Jane had organized this chocolate fondue station, which was really elegant, and, well, everything seemed a bit brighter. I really did think things were looking up.

So I'm talking to Chad, and out of the corner of my eye, I see <u>MAL</u> had the nerve to go up to <u>MY</u> <u>GRAMMY</u>. Grammy looked confused and then worried, and then she looked truly scared. I don't know what mal said to her, but she terrified her. my grammy thought that mal WAS maleficent, that she'd come to Auradon using some sort of sorcery. In that moment she must've thought she was in grave danger. When I finally went over to them, her hands were shaking and her face was pale.

I was trying to calm my grammy down, because it brought up all these horrific memories for her—poison apples and spindles and sleep spells. I'm not even sure how it happened, but the next thing I knew, that vicious Evie sprayed Chad right in the face with some sort of magic concoction!! Chad staggered back, then fell, and all those nasty villains just took off. They made a total break for it.

Honestly, I still can't believe it. Not only did Mal ruin my relationship with Ben, and ruin coronation for me, but now she's ruined Family Day. Is anything sacred?!?! When is Ben going to realize that his new "love," his new girlfriend, is nothing but trouble??

I haven't said this to anyone else, but I swear something is messed up about this. . . . Mal's been using that spell book since she got here. I would not be surprised if she spelled Ben.

FIRST OF ALL, LET'S SET THE RECORD STRAIGHT: I NEVER TRIED TO SCARE AUDREY'S GRANDMOTHER. SHE WAS THE ONE WHO CAME UP TO ME. I WAS JUST STANDING THERE, MINDING MY OWN BUSINESS, AND SHE STARTS RANTING AND RAVING ABOUT MY MOM AND FAIRIES AND POISON APPLES. (MY MOM NEVER EVEN USED POISON APPLES, BUT WHATEVER, I GUESS THAT'S BESIDE THE POINT.)

Yeah, that was MY mom. Give credit where credit's due.

THEN SHE NARROWS HER EYES AT ME, LIKE I'M THE ONE WHO RUINED HER FAMILY, AND SHE STARTS YELLING. I DID NOTHING. AND YOU KNOW WHAT?? EVEN THOUGH IT'S MY MOM, NOT ME, WHO HAS THE HISTORY WITH QUEEN LEAH, I STILL TRIED TO APOLOGIZE. NO ONE EVER WANTED TO HEAR IT.

Also, as long as we're setting the record straight, I only sprayed Chad because he pushed me, then started fighting with Jay. Someone had to step in and end it.

UGH, READING THIS NOW, YEARS LATER, BRINGS UP BAD MEMORIES. THOSE FIRST WEEKS WE WERE AT AURADON, IT WAS LIKE NOTHING WE COULD DO WAS GOOD ENOUGH. EVEN WHEN WE MADE BETTER CHOICES, NO ONE NOTICED. IT WAS USELESS.

Finally!

After Family Day my friends finally see that I was right about the villain kids— they're the nasty green mold on our otherwise perfect Auradon Prep crème brûlée. Before, everyone would tell me to give them a chance, or Lonnie and Jane would blab on and on about how great their hair looks and how they had mal to thank. But now they know. They truly know how vicious these villains can be.

That's one thing I've started doing: no more calling them "villain kids." They are VILLAINS. They grew up on the Isle of the Lost and they came here like wild animals, fighting and with <u>ZERO</u> manners, and now they're ruining <u>OUR</u> school. They've brainwashed our future king and they're plotting something, I know it.

maybe I can't prove mal spelled Ben, but I can make sure my friends stay away from her and the rest of her crew. It's only a matter of time before they self-destruct, and I'm not letting them take my friends down with them.

$\mathcal{M}$om always says if you don't feel great, try your best to LOOK great. Take a hot shower, put on a nice dress, do your hair, stand up straight, and smile. Sometimes just smiling can make you feel a little better. :)

I'm really putting her advice to the test today. It's coronation day, and Chad will be here soon to pick me up. I've done my hair and I'm in the dress I've been planning for weeks to wear, but the sadness is still following me. It's going to be so hard to see Ben and Mal come down the street in the royal coach. It'll be even worse to watch her sitting in the front row, cheering Ben on. The thought of them walking out of the cathedral together, hand in hand, celebrating after he's crowned . . .

It's too much to take. Even if she spelled him, I don't have proof. And he wouldn't want to hear it even if I did. He loves her, I keep telling myself. He loves her and he doesn't love you anymore. Just move on.

Okay. Enough of this sad, silly entry!! I have to pull myself together. Time to play the part of the ever-cool, happy-to-be-going-to-coronation-with-Chad-Charming princess. Time to impress everyone with my confidence and poise and show Ben that I DO NOT care at all about what happened at the tourney game.

Oh—Chad just knocked. I guess that's my cue. . . .

Why is everyone so surprised?!?!?

You know what? When Mal and her evil little friends grabbed Fairy Godmother's wand at the coronation, I wasn't screaming. I wasn't shocked. I just thought, Oh, right, exactly as I suspected. She's been plotting this all along.

Yeah, quick update: the only reason Mal wanted Ben to take her to the coronation was so she could sit front row, right next to Fairy Godmother's wand. I guess she had this idea that she was going to use the wand to bring down the barrier around the Isle of the Lost and free all the villains who were trapped there.

She'd been working _FOR_ her mother the whole time. They were all working for their parents. And okay, maybe mal changed her mind halfway through the plan, but that doesn't mean she didn't plan it. It's like, am I supposed to be impressed that she suddenly grew a conscience??

There was this whole
battle with her mom
(in dragon form), and
mal turned her into
a lizard and said she
and her friends chose
good now, and
<u>blah</u> <u>blah</u> <u>blah</u>.

I mean, I guess in
the moment I felt relieved it was all okay and
she did the right thing, but now that I'm back
in the dorms, I just think it's beyond twisted.
You want applause for doing the right thing?
For not using the magic wand to basically
destroy all of Auradon, a place you were
<u>INVITED</u> to because our king, my ex-boyfriend,
was kind enough to give you a second
chance?!?!?

<u>Forget that.</u> I don't know what people are thinking, but this is beyond unacceptable. If I were Ben, I'd send them all on the first limo back to the Isle of the Lost.

He's just too blinded by this infatuation, or some remaining love spell residue, to think straight.

ℰxactly one week after the coronation, nothing has changed. I kept thinking, Audrey, don't worry about it. They'll see. They'll start to think about everything mal said and did, and how she was plotting THE ENTIRE TIME she was at Auradon Prep, and everyone will realize that she's not someone they should be friends with.

Ben will realize—of course—that he shouldn't be dating her. Whatever he was feeling was a lie.

But no. Nothing has changed. I mean, just the other day, in Unsung Heroes: Sidekicks class, I heard two girls talking about how COOL it was that mal defeated her mother and chose good. How BRAVE it was that she saved everyone at the coronation. It's like, HELLO?!?!?! THE ONLY REASON THE EVIL FAIRY WHO SPELLED MY MOTHER WAS IN AURADON, FIGHTING WITH MAL, IS THAT MAL HELPED HER MOTHER GET THERE. NONE OF THIS WOULD'VE HAPPENED WITHOUT MAL. MAL IS THE COMMON THREAD HERE, WHETHER SHE SAVED THE DAY OR NOT.

It makes me so angry. My whole life, I was always told that there's nothing more important than being good. Tell the truth, don't steal or cheat, always follow the rules. I mean, what's the point if no one REALLY cares?!?!

mal didn't follow the rules. mal does MAGIC even though it's ILLEGAL in Auradon, and Ben hasn't made a peep about it. mal used a LOVE SPELL to steal my boyfriend and make a fool of me in front of the entire school, and it's like it didn't even happen. All anyone is talking about is the coronation and how MAL chose good and saved the day—not that she lied to us and was plotting to take down our entire kingdom.

I just . . . I can't deal with it anymore. It's so unfair. The more I think about it, the more I'm certain: fairy tales don't come true. Good doesn't always conquer evil. Because what mal was doing these past few weeks, while Ben looked the other way?? That was truly evil.

So I made some really big mistakes. I admit it. Audrey has a point that I went about everything the wrong way. But I fell in love with Ben. I really did. And in that moment at the coronation, I knew I could never go through with my mom's plot.

I learned. I grew. Doesn't that count for something?

You cannot keep beating yourself up about this. Trust me—there are enough people in this world who are going to try to tear you down; you don't have to do that to yourself. Villains gonna villain, it's as simple as that. You were doing what you were raised to do, what you were told to do every single day of your villainous life.

I'm tired of feeling sorry for being who I am. I want to be better, and I will be, but I'm done apologizing.

Do you know how long it's been since the day of the tourney game??? Of course you don't—you're a diary—but I do. It's been <u>exactly 36 days.</u>

It's not even like I've been intentionally counting the days, checking my calendar, or anything. It's more that each day feels so long, and I keep waiting for things to change, like suddenly Ben is going to show up at my dorm and announce that he finally knows he made a mistake. He finally realizes how horrible it was that he started singing to mal at that game. That he chose her over me.

I keep waiting, but it never happens.

And every time I see him and mal in the

quad, laughing and having a good time, or

every time I see Jane going over some event

with mal, asking her what SHE thinks of the

flowers or decor,

I just . . . it hurts

so badly.

It's all a

reminder that it's

over. Ben and

I might truly

be done.

Chad has been such a good friend to me lately. It's made things a little easier, but not much. I mean, at least I have someone to eat lunch with and walk through the halls with, and it doesn't <u>SEEM</u> like I'm thinking about Ben all the time. But I guess what does it really matter if I am? If I can't get him out of my mind?

I keep thinking about all the good times we've had together over the years. Like how we dressed up as Princess Aurora and the Beast on Ancestry Day, and how we won the three-legged race at last year's Auradon Games. I was so determined to win I was racing as fast as I could, and I was somehow even faster than Ben, and right as we were closing in on the finish line, he fell over. I had to drag him over the line! Then we both fell down laughing in the grass. We laughed so hard there were tears in our eyes.

Or the days we'd go riding in Sherwood Forest. I've been riding horses since I was a kid, and so has Ben, and it's something we always did _together_. We'd weave through the trees and then stop in one of the clearings for a picnic. Then we'd ride all the way back, chatting about school or what it would be like to be an official royal couple one day. It was so easy to be with him.

I can't think of it, though. I can't anymore. I have to push all those happy memories aside. I keep telling myself that if Ben wants to be with Mal, then he's definitely not the guy for me, and I'm hoping that at some point soon I'll really _believe_ it.

I just wish it didn't still hurt. . . .

After school today Chad and I went down to Belle's Harbor, because I've been in a terrible mood lately and he thought it might cheer me up. He was telling me this story about his weekend in the Summerlands and how he can water-ski on one leg, and it was so silly and charming that for a few brief moments I forgot all about Ben, and Mal, and everything that's happened since the coronation.

We walked along the shore and were reminiscing about spending afternoons in Chad's parents' castle when we were growing up, and about how Auradon used to be before all this villain nonsense. <u>Then we saw them</u>. Ben and Mal were sitting on the edge of the dock with their feet in the water. Mal had her head on Ben's shoulder and they were talking and laughing and watching the sunset together. They didn't even notice we were there.

Chad steered me away and we took the long way back, through the city. He just started in on another story. This one was about Jaq trying to move this huge wheel of cheese, even though Jaq weighs like .0002 pounds, so it was useless. I couldn't stop thinking about Ben and Mal sitting there, and how that was supposed to be ME. I was supposed to be dating Ben. I was supposed to be in line to be queen.

I don't know who I was kidding. I can't spend another week, another month, watching Ben and Mal play out their fairy tale. I don't want to see them in the halls or on the quad or at the picnic tables, staring at each other with hearts in their eyes. This weekend is my annual spa retreat with Flora, Fauna, and Merryweather. My mom and I usually go to their fairy cottage in the woods and spend a few days with them. This year I'm going to ask my mom if I can stay for a while. I mean, I'm ahead in all my classes, and the fairies homeschooled her for years.

I need a break from Auradon Prep, from everything. The Fairy Cottage has always been a place where I can truly be myself. I think some time there might be good for me.

At least I hope so.

Ahhhhhhh.

That is the sound of someone who is finally away from Auradon Prep and all the complete nonsense it has come to represent. That is the sound of me **RELAXING** and **ENJOYING** life again. That is the sound of forgetting.

At my mother's christening, Flora gave her the gift of beauty. But if I've learned anything from my dear fairy godmother, it's that beauty can mean many things, and above all else, being beautiful is about **FEELING** beautiful. We started our annual spa vacation with some honey and oatmeal facials. Then we soaked our feet in a lovely sea salt soak with some rosemary sprigs to make it smell good. We must've sat there for hours, our heads back on pillows, our eyes covered with cold cucumber. We were quiet, and we just enjoyed how <u>peaceful</u> it was.

Fauna wants to take me to get a manicure and pedicure in a bit. We'll have to go into town for that. It feels so good to be here, in the middle of the woods, with my godmothers. I really feel like myself here, and it's been so relaxing that Auradon Prep is starting to seem like a dream (or nightmare, really) that I've finally woken up from.

The best thing about being here with my fairy godmothers is that it's EASY. Simple. You know how when you're at dinner with your parents, they pepper you with all these questions and want to know how you're doing in school, and how your friends are, and they're giving you advice and all that? It's not like that with Flora, Fauna, and merryweather. And it's not that they don't care about me—they do, a lot. That's not it at all. maybe it's because they're older and they already raised my mom for almost sixteen years, but they've gotten really mellow. They sit and relax with me, and they let ME do the talking.

No questions or expectations. We just enjoy each other and stay in the present moment.

I've been here three days already and they haven't asked me about what happened with Ben, or why I haven't mentioned him. They're following my lead. I'm going to tell them eventually (though I'm sure Grammy and mom already did, if they somehow didn't see it on the news). For now I'm just . . . letting it all <u>sink in</u>.

Lilies of the Valley

Sugar Scrub Pedicure

Sugar Scrub Manicure

Pumpkin Spice Facial

Blueberry and Thyme Facial

Fairy Haircut
twelve faires included in price

Fairy Hair Coloring
six fairies included in price

It's been really nice here.
Every morning Fauna and I take a stroll
through the woods and sing while we walk.
Sometimes we make up little songs, and
sometimes we'll sing the songs she sang to
my mother when she was a kid. We stop and
pick flowers or find a nice log to sit on and let
the birds join our songs.

It's hard to think about anything when
you're singing, you know? You lose yourself
in the moment. The rest of the world
goes away.

I went back to Lilies of the valley today alone. I'd been thinking about getting a new look for a while, and it seemed like as good a time as any. One of the amazing things about getting your hair done there is that they'll put twelve fairies on your haircut, and they swarm around your head, each with her own little pair of scissors. They grab a strand or two and work on that for a while, and then they put the color in with these miniature paintbrushes. They all communicate the whole time, whispering back and forth to each other, or calling out random things like "SHORTER!!" or "TOO BRIGHT!!!" to create a unified look. I decided to add two more fairies (it costs a little extra, but whatever) so the process would go even faster. In less than an hour, I was completely transformed.

Okay, so if I'm being completely honest, I was a little influenced by mal's style. Or maybe it's just "Isle style"—can mal really take <u>all</u> the credit for it? Ever since what happened at the tourney game, I've wondered if maybe I play it a little safe with my hair and my outfits and everything. I mean, I'm still waaaaaay better than mal, and Ben made a huge mistake by dumping me, but I thought maybe I <u>COULD</u> play up my personality a bit more with my fashion and hair. Why not try something new?

The fairies ended up putting light blue and pink highlights throughout my hair. I think it really brightens up my look. Afterward, I went into Camelot Heights with Merryweather and found an outfit at a small boutique there. When I tried it on, I couldn't stop staring at my reflection in the mirror. I look so different . . . I look really _COOL_.

I can't wait until Ben sees me like this—when I stroll back onto the Auradon Prep quad, head held high, and he realizes what a fool he's been. I'm not going to make him beg me to take him back—that would be cruel—

but I'm definitely going to make him wait.
Like, I wouldn't just be all, "Of course, Ben!
We can start dating again!!" I may have to
take just a day or two to think about it. :)

The only reason my parents agreed to let me stay here with my fairy godmothers is that they're teaching me a lot of things like they did for my mom. My mom knows all about the fairies' wisdom. They taught her everything for sixteen years of her life, and my mom is one of the smartest and most well-read people I know. (So much of her fairy tale is about that spindle and her sleeping through the curse, that they don't get to show who she REALLY is as a person. It's a little frustrating.)

So I've been spending time with my fairy godmothers instead of at Auradon Prep. They decided to cover some of the same curriculum I had at Auradon Prep. They got all the supplemental materials from Fairy Godmother. We've already cruised through Safety Rules for the Internet. Now we're on to Virtues and Values.

This just in: grammar is as boring when your sweet fairy godmothers teach it as it is when you take it at Auradon Prep. I know it's part of having good manners, but I seriously cannot hear any more about present perfect tense! It's like, I GET IT!!

I can't even count how many lectures my mom gave me in her restaurant about tricking people into bad deals. she must've told me thousands of times that the most important thing in life was taking something meaningful away from someone else. (Reality check: that's not true.)

Yeah, villainous lectures are a little different. Mom was so focused on teaching me how to manipulate, lie, and cheat my way to success we didn't get to any of the more basic stuff . . . like the ABCS and addition and subtraction. Fortunately, dragon Hall was there for that.

I made a really big mistake this morning. <u>Huge</u>. After Fauna and I went on our early stroll through the forest, she ducked into the kitchen to make tea. It's been so relaxing in the woods I've barely spoken to any of my friends back at Auradon Prep, and I suddenly had the strange urge to see what was going on with them.

merryweather has a small television in her room that she has always let me use, so I went upstairs and turned on the Auradon News Network. Just writing this,

I feel my stomach twisting into knots. There, on the screen, were Ben and Mal. THEY WERE EATING LUNCH WITH ALADDIN AND JASMINE. Then there was this whole segment on the Royal Cotillion, how that's coming up in the next few weeks and everyone can't wait to see what MAL is going to wear.

What MAL is going to wear!! I can't even believe it. I was sure they would've broken up by now, but no, Ben has been taking her all over the United States of Auradon on this huge grand tour, introducing her to every hero in the land. Every time Mal is on TV, she's in some sparkling new dress, commenting on this or that happening around Auradon Prep.

People aren't supposed to be talking about what <u>MAL</u>'s wearing, they're supposed to be talking about what <u>I'm</u> wearing. <u>I'm</u> supposed to be there at those lunches with Ben, telling Aladdin stories about growing up in the castle.

<u>I'm</u> supposed to be doing a costume change every three hours and giving comments to the <u>Auradon Gazette</u>.

That's supposed to be <u>me</u>.

It's like she didn't just steal my boyfriend—she stole my future. <u>my entire life</u>.

Wow. Of course I hated being on TV that much in the first weeks Ben and I were dating. It always felt so forced and uncomfortable. But I can see now what it must've been like for Audrey, watching from miles away.

We were everywhere. Camerapeople and reporters were always following us around and putting new articles and segments online and on TV. People were obsessed. Even if Audrey hadn't been looking for us, she would've been confronted by our smiling faces every time she turned on the TV.

IT MUST'VE BEEN TORTURE.

I haven't even turned
on the television since the other day, and I
don't want to ever watch it again. Grammy
has already started hinting that it might
be time for me to go back to Auradon
Prep, that maybe my little retreat in
the woods should come to an end soon.
She doesn't want me missing any of the
advanced courses at Auradon Prep that

I need to take to get into a good college. (The fairies can do pretty much anything, but they aren't certified to teach advanced placement classes.)

I know I can't stay here forever, but if that's what's going on at Auradon Prep, count me out. I'm not going back there just so I can be an audience for mal and Ben's love story.

What's that phrase again??

It's like <u>SALT</u> <u>IN</u> <u>A</u> <u>WOUND.</u>

It still burns, it still hurts.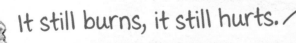

I really was planning on going to Cotillion. making a big entrance with my edgy new look and wowing everyone. I loved the idea of it stealing even a little bit of the spotlight away from Ben and Mal. If my parents were going to make me go back at some point, I wanted to at least decide WHEN.

Flora, Fauna, and Merryweather helped me get into my dress and do my hair. They wanted to actually go in the carriage with me and escort me to the dance, but I told them no. (Can you imagine how babyish it would've looked, me showing up with my three godmothers in tow?) So I started off through the woods, directing the horses to Belle's Harbor, where the yacht was docked, and trying not to think about how they stole my idea for using it for Auradon Prep events. I was halfway there, just at the border of Auradon City itself, when I got a flat tire.

I didn't want to worry my grammy or my godmothers, so I ended up calling Chad to get me. Even after all these months apart, he still jumped at the opportunity to see me again. I mean, I get the sense he might've thought we were **REALLY** dating (not just together to make Ben jealous), but I can't be responsible for that.

Anyway, he was there in less than six hours, and he fixed the tire on my carriage and took me back to the Fairy Cottage, and even helped get some of the mud off my skirt. The whole time he was repairing the axle, he didn't once mention Ben or Mal. In fact, he didn't say anything about them the whole ride home, or when he sat with us at the kitchen table and had Fauna's special fig cake. He just said that he was happy to see me and was hoping I'd be back at Auradon Prep soon, and that he'd missed hanging out.

Oh, Chad. I know he's handsome and charming and all that, but he's just not for me. At least I can always count on him to come through for me, though. Lately it feels like he's the <u>only person</u> at Auradon Prep who remembers I exist. . . .

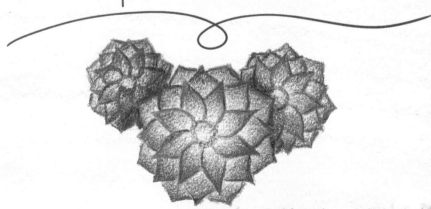

First day back. My family is here at the Fairy Cottage, and they've already packed up all my stuff in the back of the carriage. There's no use arguing with them anymore. If I have to be at Auradon Prep again, I'm determined not to let Mal and all her friends ruin it for me.

I mean, I was there before them.

It's <u>**MY**</u> school, <u>not theirs.</u>

I'm not going to pretend like I wasn't a little bit nervous walking into Auradon Prep again after being away. Lumiere and Cogsworth took all my bags up to my room so that I could work on settling in. I walked into the cafeteria to get breakfast and just acted like I'd never left. This group of girls in line started <u>oohing</u> and <u>aahing</u> over my hair. They must've complimented me a dozen times on my new outfit, too.

That definitely boosted my confidence. Even if Mal and Ben are still together, now that I'm back it's only a matter of time before they break up. I mean, I saw how uncomfortable Mal looked when she was eating dinner with Aladdin and Jasmine. Ben must've noticed, too. Her manners aren't nearly as polished as they need to be for her to be queen, and I'm sure they're running into problems, with her trying to lead people as a villain and all. How <u>embarrassing</u>— for Ben and for all of the kingdom.

I **FINALLY** ran into Ben this afternoon. It was perfect timing, because he was alone, sitting by Beast's statue out front. I still remember how he turned and smiled when he saw me. He was like, "Audrey! I'm glad you're back!" And then he stood and gave me a <u>big</u> <u>hug</u>.

Then he complimented me on my new hair <u>AND</u> my new boots. He thought they were really cool. I was so stunned I think I just smiled and nodded, but inside, my heart was exploding. It confirmed all these things I'd been thinking and feeling for so long.

I know he still cares about me. I know it. Why else would he compliment me??

Unbelievable.

Truly unbelievable. I've only been back three days, and everywhere I go, kids are talking about how "cool" mal and her friends are, and how they love Evie's 4 Hearts dresses, and how cute Jane and Carlos are as a couple. I mean, even Doug has started dating a villain!! DOUG!!!

Has everyone completely forgotten about how mal SPELLED our King and plotted to steal Fairy Godmother's wand?? Or how she wanted to bring down the barrier and unleash total chaos over the realm?? She's not to be trusted. It doesn't matter if Ben is dating her, or if Evie can sew great formal

dresses. Who cares if Jay is one of the best players on the tourney team?!?
The future and safety of Auradon is the most important thing. We have to protect that, and we have to see these kids for what they really are: VILLAINS!!

I'm just plain old disappointed in Lonnie and Jane. It's like as soon as I left, they just replaced me with Mal, cloning her style and adoring her the way they used to adore me. I thought they had better taste than that. Guess not.

I get it, I do. We went about things the wrong way when we first got to Auradon. We still had our parents' voices in our heads telling us to be bad, to plot and manipulate and lie. To steal Fairy Godmother's wand and do things that are against the kingdom. But things are different now—I'm different.

I walked into the cafeteria today, and both Jane and Lonnie were sitting with the villains. They were laughing and chatting and having a blast. If they think I'm going to join in, they're madder than a hatter.

But it was weird, because for the first time in my entire life, I was one of those kids looking around, trying to figure out where I was going to sit. Fortunately, Chad was on the other side of the cafeteria and it didn't take long for him to spot me and wave me over. But still. Has everyone else forgotten I'm the popular one??

Don't they understand that every minute they spend with Mal or Carlos or Evie or Jay is a complete betrayal? I am furious. It's like my friendship meant nothing to Jane and Lonnie. They forgot about me faster than you can say bibbidi-bobbidi-boo. All those sleepovers in my castle turret, and being each other's valentines, and studying for the mermaid Language exams together. What's the point of investing time making friends if they're not going to be loyal to you?! So. Rude.

I've actually talked to Jane about this. In her defense, she always felt like Audrey took their friendship for granted. Jane was always checking in with Audrey, asking her how she was or getting her birthday presents or whatever, and Audrey wasn't great at reciprocating. I could totally see that—Jane's so thoughtful and generous and sweet. I think even Carlos has a hard time keeping up.

Mal and Ben are EVERYWHERE. What's worse is that this isn't the Auradon News Network, this is real life. There's no OFF button. There's no way to just avoid them or pretend they don't exist. Every time I turn a corner or walk across the quad, they're right there, right in front of me, holding hands. Smiling at each other with googly eyes.

Also—I guess this is a bigger deal—Jane wasn't always her best self around Audrey. Audrey was always trying to get Jane to say mean things to us or "put us in our place." Jane knew it was wrong, but she said she was feeling a lot of pressure to fit in. I honestly can't imagine her now saying or doing any of the things she did months ago when she was friends with Audrey.

The most humiliating thing happened today. I was walking down one of the outdoor hallways up on the second floor by the science wing, and I spotted Ben. I was about to go over to him, because he was alone (for once) and I thought maybe we could talk or catch up. His back was turned toward me, and he had his hand in his backpack. It took me a minute to realize what he was doing.

HE WAS LEAVING A NOTE IN MAL'S LOCKER.

I watched the whole thing. Just stood there frozen, like some statue from the Auradon Museum of Cultural History. He slipped the note inside the little metal opening and then walked away with the biggest smile on his face. I've seen him and Mal eating lunch before, or studying together in the library, but now he's leaving notes in her locker???

I thought that was <u>OUR</u> thing.

It's like she's completely replaced me.

I don't even know where to start. I'm still trying to get used to mal and her villainous, conniving friends being here in _MY_ city. At _MY_ school. (who am I kidding? I won't ever get used to it.) Then today Chad found me on the quad and told me the news. Apparently Evie has convinced Ben to allow even more villains into Auradon Prep. __FOUR__ __MORE__. Before you know it, the entire school will be infested with them.

The thing is this doesn't seem like Ben's idea. His bringing mal and her friends to Auradon might've worked out for his love life, but anyone who watched the coronation knows that it wasn't a good idea. Do these kids really deserve a spot at Auradon Prep?

Chad and I were discussing it, and the more I think about it, the more it seems like Ben's still under some sort of spell. Maybe Evie spelled him this time, or maybe they put something in his cologne to make him easier to influence. Like a listening spell or something? A persuasion spell?

I'm sure there's another devious plot to uncover. Mal is still up to something, I just know it.

As if it weren't bad enough that Ben invited all these rotten kids to our school, now he's made going to the welcome party MANDATORY. Everyone has to show up on the quad this afternoon to greet the new recruits. Even Grammy is coming in for it.

He keeps telling people there'll be a big surprise, and it'll be worth it, but nothing he could do or say would make it worth it. Why is the focus always on the villain kids, and reforming the villain kids, and which villain kids they're planning on bringing over next? What happened to the days when being

GOOD was rewarded? When heroes reigned and royalty was respected? I understand Ben wanted to switch things up a bit, and citizens are excited about young blood on the throne, but there's such a thing as taking it too far.

I guess I have to go get ready . . .

TO SMILE AND CHEER AND GREET THESE NEW VILLAINS, WHO WILL PROBABLY MAKE EVERYTHING THAT MUCH WORSE.

*O*h, a great surprise!!! Something that would make going to the welcome gathering worth it!! YOU KNOW WHAT THAT SURPRISE WAS???? YOU KNOW WHAT BEN DECIDED TO DO IN FRONT OF THE ENTIRE KINGDOM???

PROPOSE TO MAL.
    HE DECIDED TO PROPOSE TO MAL.

AND SHE SAID YES.

I'm so furious right now my hands are shaking. You would've thought he'd finally learned his lesson from the tourney game and how utterly humiliating that was for me, to be dumped in front of the entire school. But no. This afternoon I had to stand there and watch as he pulled a ring from his pocket, got down on one knee, and asked Mal to

marry him. He'd handed out all these signs
to the audience ahead of time, so as soon
as she said yes, people flipped them around.
Everywhere I turned, it said CONGRATS! and
QUEEN MAL and HAPPILY EVER AFTER.
  And there was a live feed of their friends
and family and everything.

  It was like my dreams were all coming true,
but they were coming true for someone else . . .
for someone who is not even a good person.
Mal is living the life I always wanted. How is
  this <u>fair</u> or <u>okay</u>?!

It's midnight and I think it's only now really hitting me: Ben and I will never be together. He loves mal. He's marrying mal.

mal is the one who's going to be queen.

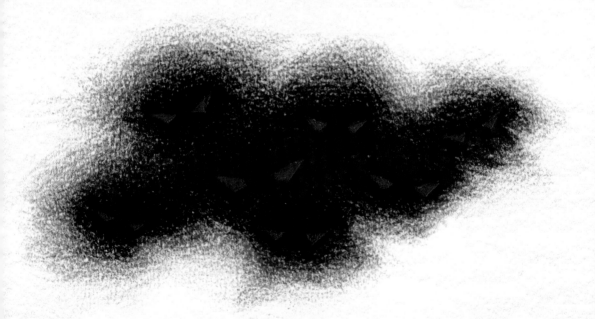

I didn't ask for this. I never wanted to be in magazines or all over the Auradon News Network. I never wanted to do these lunches with heroes across the nineteen regions. It just kind of happened. I fell in love with Ben, and this was what came with it.

I guess what I'm trying to say is I never set out to steal Audrey's dream. Even when I spelled Ben, it wasn't because I wanted him to be in love with me—it was because I needed him to be in love with me. It was all about getting Fairy Godmother's wand.

Falling for Ben? That was just a happy accident that came with it. It was all out of my control.

SNAP!
That's cold,
Grammy!!

It's like my grammy's voice is playing on repeat. I keep hearing those words <u>over</u> and <u>over</u> again—everything she said to me at the welcome gathering after Ben proposed to mal. She looked at me with such disappointment in her eyes. Then she shook her head. "A lifetime of plans, gone. Our family status, gone. You let him slip through your fingers! <u>Your mother could hold on to a prince in her sleep!</u>" She raised her voice when she said that last part, and I'm certain the people around us heard her.

Now they all know what a failure I am.

Everyone says my grandmother hasn't been the same since the sleeping spell and what maleficent put her through. I know my mom and dad would tell me she was just angry and she didn't really know what she was saying. But how can I unhear it?? How <u>can</u> I <u>forget</u>??

Besides, it's always been there, this expectation that Ben and I were going to date and eventually get married. my parents always wanted me to become queen; it was so obvious. They were the most excited when Ben and I started dating. They asked me practically every day how things were, and if we were in love, and where I saw it going.

They've always known that our marrying
would bring more attention to South Riding
and Auroria. If we wed, our two families
would form an unbreakable alliance. We were
supposed to lead Auradon together—that
was always the plan.

And now what? What am I if I'm not
THE QUEEN?

I've disappointed my entire family, and
there's no way for me to make it better.
There's nothing I can say or do to turn
this around. I can't go back . . . but how
am I supposed to go forward?? How can
I possibly move on when living in Auradon
means living under **MY ENEMY'S** rule?!?

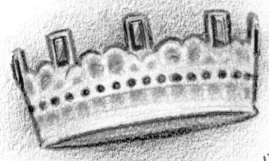

I'm so tired of pretending. Where's my happy ending?!?!

If they want a villain for a queen, I'm going
to be one like they've never seen. . . .

Nave

Gallery

Gallery of
Villains

The History
of magic

Hall of Caves

Hall of Scrolls

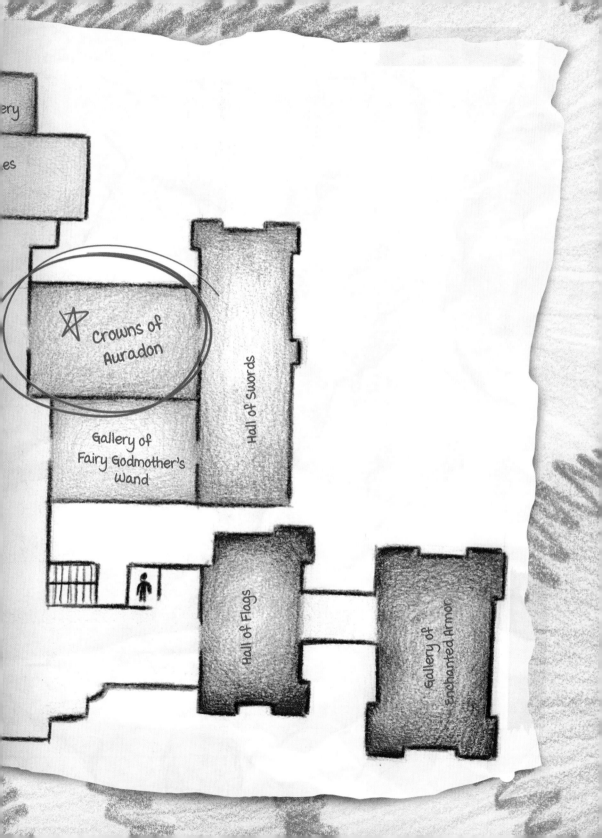

I only went to the Auradon Museum of Cultural History to steal the crown. I just wanted to feel the weight of it on my head . . . to DECLARE MYSELF a queen. But when I got there, maleficent's scepter called to me. I could feel its dark power and all it could do for me . . . how it could change my life.

I wanted it. I needed it. . . .

$\mathcal{P}$oor unsuspecting mal was coming out of Evie's starter castle when I surprised her. Hahaha! You should've seen her face when she saw me standing there with a crown on my head and her mother's scepter in my grasp. She'd never seemed so powerless before. Her mouth dropped open in a sad little O. "Wait, Audrey, stop, don't use that," she begged. She kept yapping on about it being dangerous and not a toy.

Please.

She knows she doesn't have long. I'M the QUEEN now. The POWER is mine. I can feel it coursing through my veins. I wasn't sure what it was I saw in mal's eyes right then and there, that strange expression she had,

but now I know: SHE WAS AFRAID OF ME.
It felt good that for once, she was the one
groveling ... she was the one worried
   and sad. ...

I had to show her some of my new powers,
right? I couldn't just walk away and pretend
   like everything was normal between us,
could I? The scepter surged in my hand, and
   I thought of all she's taken from me, all she
has STOLEN, and the ugliness she's shown me
   and my family. I turned her into a hideous
witch!! Wrinkled, withered face and long
gray hair!! A hunched back and torn cloak.
And I laughed and laughed and laughed
   as I did it. ....

Yeah ... That was
NOT COOl.

If the old Audrey hadn't been invited to a party, she would've just sat around in her dorm room feeling sad. She would've worried about everyone having fun without her and wondered if she hadn't been invited for a reason, and she would've started thinking about Mal and Ben and everything she'd had and lost. The old Audrey would've cried.

BUT NOT THE NEW AUDREY. THE NEW AUDREY GETS REVENGE.

I found an invitation to Jane's birthday party on the ground outside the castle. You remember Jane, my ex-best friend who turned into a mal-worshipping villain lover?? Well, she didn't think to invite me to her little celebration. Apparently I'm not <u>GOOD</u> enough anymore.

(<u>Hahaha.</u> It feels good not to be good.)

I can't wait to make her regret that decision. . . .

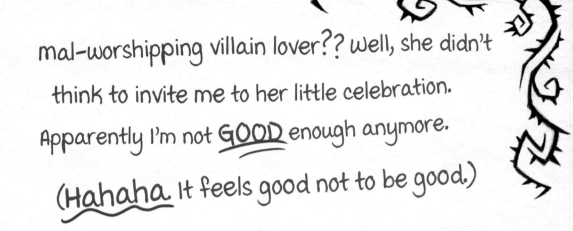

Please join us in celebrating

Jane's birthday!

When
On Jane's birthday, of course!

Where
The Enchanted Lake

How should I get my revenge?

That's the question I ask now.
Instead of sitting around and
wondering <u>why</u> Ben didn't choose me,
or <u>why</u> everyone's forgotten what
mal did to our kingdom, now I ask:

<u>What</u> will I do to make them pay??
<u>How</u> will I make them sorry??
<u>How</u> can I crush their spirits the
way they crushed mine?!?

I can't wait to make my grand
entrance at Jane's party. . . .

Ways to Ruin Jane's Birthday

—Blast her cake into a thousand pieces

—make it rain and thunder and lightning so everyone is soaked

—Turn Jane's hair bright green (That might backfire—green hair is a bit stylish these days.)

—Turn Carlos into a dog

—Or even better . . . take a cue from maleficent. Who doesn't love a sleep spell?

z z Z z z Z z z Z Z

Jane had her birthday picnic at the Enchanted Lake, and I appeared in a cloud of smoke, my scepter glowing with power. It felt divine to unleash all my anger on those Auradon Prep fools. "You mindless drones!" I yelled. "How could you forget what she tried to do to us? How could you forget that I was supposed to be your queen??"

They finally listened to me. They sat there, silent, and for the very first time heard what I had to say, all the things I'd been trying to tell them for so long. They wanted an evil ruler??

WELL, NOW THEY HAVE ONE!!!

I laughed and laughed as I cast the sleep spell. The fog descended on them and they drifted off like babies. Let them understand what it is to have your life slip through your fingers. Let them know what it means to have hours, then days, then years <u>stolen</u> from you.

LET THEM KNOW WHAT MY MOTHER FELT.

LET THEM KNOW. . . .

I grew up hearing stories about my mother's scepter and all the power it has. That's why it was so TERRIFYING when I saw it in Audrey's hands, taking her over.

I'm sure Audrey really was angry and hurt that she wasn't invited to Jane's birthday party. But when she was holding the scepter, everything was magnified. Because it wasn't just her thoughts and her emotions coming to the surface. All the rage and fury my mother felt at not being invited to Aurora's christening was channeled through her. Hurt and anger from decades ago is STRONGER than ever before, and the WORST part is now the scepter has a new person to unleash it. It's a powerful and dangerous object— maybe the most powerful and dangerous in all of Auradon.

What a beautiful sight it is, the fog rolling out over Auradon. It takes down whoever comes in contact with it—the old and the young, the rich and the poor. Villains and heroes alike.

Lately the streets are so quiet I can hear my heels clicking on the pavement. Half of Auradon is asleep. They are under my spell. . . .

I don't even have to worry about seeing Mal and Ben being all cutesy on the Auradon News Network anymore. Every single reporter is only talking about one thing: ME. They're wondering why people are saying that I'M behind the sleeping spell. They're wondering if it could be true.

This one reporter was on camera, telling everyone about the fog, and he was all, "We have an update! It's moving this way! It's moving . . ."
Then it enveloped him and he completely passed out. Hahaha.
I love seeing my spell in action. . . .

THE REPORTERS DIDN'T THINK AUDREY
WAS REALLY THE ONE WHO'D DONE THIS—AT FIRST
THEY WERE LOOKING FOR A VILLAIN
TO BLAME. IF I'VE LEARNED
ANYTHING FROM AUDREY, IT'S
THAT EVERYONE HAS
THEIR SECRETS.
EVEN THE MOST
"PERFECT" PEOPLE
ARE PRETENDING
IN SOME WAY,
OR HURTING
IN SOME WAY, OR
THEY HAVE SOMETHING
THEY'RE TRYING TO HIDE
FROM THE REST OF THE
WORLD.

AUDREY DID THIS BECAUSE
SHE'D BOTTLED UP ALL HER
FEELINGS—HELD THEM IN UNTIL THEY RUSHED OUT IN A
BIG, UGLY MESS. I'VE MADE MY OWN MISTAKES, AND
I GET IT—WHAT IT'S LIKE NOT TO SAY WHAT YOU
FEEL AND THEN JUST ACT.

Now they're passing out gas masks at the castle. They're trying to give them to as many citizens as possible before the fog sweeps through every neighborhood. I've heard there's a limited supply . . . haha. . . .

They can try as hard as they want. They'll never be able to stop me.

Already people are being drawn to my <u>power</u>. They're signing up to be my sidekicks, my lackeys. They'll do anything they can to endear themselves to me.

Right before I cast the sleep spell at Jane's party, Chad ran away from the rest of those ungrateful heroes' kids and begged me to spare him. He told me he'd do anything to help me. For a little while I really did think that I could replace Ben with Chad, that Chad's friendship might be enough to make it all stop hurting.

~~~ I was wrong.

Chad Charming will never be enough for me. But just like when he came to help me in Sherwood Forest, I can rely on him now to do whatever I need him to do. "Fetch me a tea," I say, and poof!! It's there. "Go find out why Uma is in Auradon," I say, and he'll spend hours on his phone, trying to track exactly where she is and what she's doing. No, Chad's not enough—he's not smart enough, he's not powerful enough, HE'S NOT BEN. But I will put him to good use. ~~~

Welcome to my wicked world, where anything is possible. ANYTHING. When I stare into the orb on top of my scepter, I can see people and places in all of Auradon, glimpses of my expansive realm. I watched Mal lead Uma and her pirate crew through the city streets, and I saw them heading to the castle. But sometimes I use the orb for other things . . . like to see all those silly little heroes passed out around the Enchanted Lake. Sometimes it's nice to remind myself what I'm capable of. I've already conquered so many.

That's not all I can do, though. . . .
I can control my surroundings . . .
spell objects and make them mine.

I hurl them around the room, a tornado
of chaos. Rolling pins. Furniture. Picture
frames. I can blast stone sculptures
apart and disappear in clouds of
thick pink smoke.

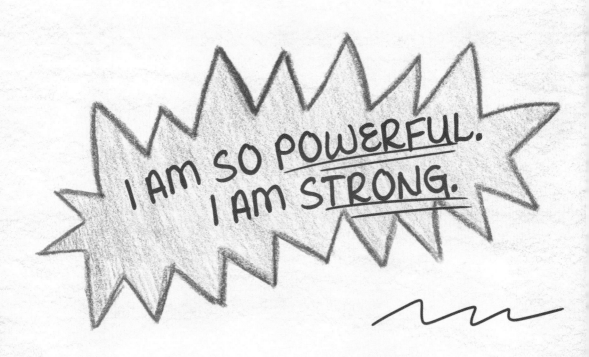

This is my castle now, and I won't have any TRESPASSERS. mal might think she belongs here, but SHE WILL NEVER BELONG HERE. She will never have royal blood coursing through her veins. She will never know what it feels like to have MY CROWN on her head. I am the queen now, NO ONE ELSE, and she will never again take what's mine.

They thought they could just stroll right through the castle gates and not be punished. Fortunately, I trapped them in the hall of armor. I spelled those silver knight suits and had them defend what's <u>rightfully</u> mine. I loved watching the VKs scatter like mice. I loved seeing how afraid they were, how small they seemed compared to <u>MY ARMY</u>, <u>MY POWER</u>....

<u>RIGHT</u>...
Reading this, you'd think we didn't defeat her sad army of tin men.

She can TRY TO REWRITE HISTORY, but we all know what happened—we were all there. We TURNED THOSE GHOST KNIGHTS INTO SCRAP METAL.

I'll admit it, UMa, I wasn't sure how it was going to be, trying to lead our crews together. I was yelling for people to go right and you were yelling for people to go left. I wanted us to advance when you wanted us to fall back. But as soon as we started talking ("COMMUNICATING" ... isn't that the fancy, touchy-feely word??), we were UNSTOPPABLE.

It's weird we've been enemies for so long. I can't help thinking of all we could've done on the Isle if we'd been working together.

Good! This is good!!
This is real progress. I'm telling you you
should still do some exercises saying
things you like about each other.
I think it could really help.

Do you hear this, Mal???
Evie's going to have us doing
trust falls soon. Ha.
But yeah, what happened in the castle was cool.
Turns out we make a good team.

Remember what Fairy Godmother says:
it's easy to be a queen among paupers,
but it's hard to be a queen among queens.

We're all queens here. We just need to
figure out how to support each other and
work with each other's strengths. I think
we're off to a good start, right?

Ben walks the halls of Auradon Prep like he did nothing wrong. Like that tourney game never happened. Like he didn't HUMILIATE ME and RUIN MY LIFE.

I wanted to make sure I came up with something truly special for him. A spell unlike any other. Sure, I thought about your ordinary, run-of-the-mill magic—turning him into a frog, gifting him a poison apple, blasting his crown into a thousand pieces. But none of it seemed right. What is Ben most afraid of?? What are his weaknesses?? His insecurities??

I had to think a while back, but I remembered . . . it did eventually come to me. . . .

"I'm afraid everyone will think I'm like my father—how he was before," he said to me one day when we were in sixth grade. We were sitting in the West Wing, and Ben had just stopped to show me the old scratches on the wall. The ones his dad had put there many, many years before. "I'm afraid that somehow I'll be transformed into a beast. I'll be angry and mean and no one will love me. It's silly, I know. . . ."

IT'S NOT SILLY, BENNY BOO. IT'S KIND OF PERFECT.

What better way to make him feel small and alone and scared?? To make him feel UNLOVED??

With one blast of my scepter, I destroyed that pretty boy shell of his and made him look like an overgrown dog. He was bumbling around the school and the castle, growling and snarling and stomping his massive paws. He let out a great roar of anger.

I LOVED EVERY MINUTE OF IT.

How does it feel, Ben, to know you'll never have the life you want?? To know everyone is laughing at you?? Do you understand that you're nothing now, that you will always be nothing?!?!

NO ONE WILL EVER LOVE YOU!!

There's nothing Audrey could do to make me stop loving Ben. That's not how love works. You don't stop caring for someone just because they turn into a beast, or start ROARRRRing or whatever.

In fact, I kind of like Ben's new look. I call it Beast after a splash from the Enchanted Lake. The long hair . . . the furry chest . . . Okay, if I'm being completely honest, I'm not so crazy about the tail. Hopefully it's not a permanent thing, but if I have to live with it, I will.

I saw my chance as soon as the VKs slipped into Evie's castle. Maybe they were able to fight off my knights, but I knew it was only a matter of time before they were overcome by my power. I raised my scepter and closed my eyes, feeling the intensity swirling through me. Broken logs and scattered wood rushed out of the depths of the forest. The pieces flew through the air.

WHAP! WHAP! WHAP!

Planks boarded up each window, one by one, trapping the VKs inside.

They screamed and yelled and I laughed and laughed, thinking I finally had them where I wanted them. I heard their pathetic whimpers inside. But then I saw something in my orb . . . something strange. Mal tried to break free of my trap using her magic, but she couldn't. So Uma, daughter of Ursula, stepped forward and held her shell necklace up in front of her. They started chanting together and combining their powers to try to defeat me. Somehow it worked, because the wood planks blasted away from the castle and they were free.

I'm not impressed by it—not at all. I've escaped to the Fairy Cottage to plot my next move, but I'm chalking that victory up to LUCK. Not talent, not skill. LUCK!!

If they're stronger together, I will just have to be more powerful, more evil, more merciless. . . . Next time THEY WON'T STAND A CHANCE. . . .

She can "chalk it" (whatever that means) any way she wants, but the truth is we kicked her butt. She tried to trap us in Evie's castle and she failed, because we used Mal's spell and my shell necklace and all the energy of Hades's ember.

When I saw how fast those boards flew off the windows, how crazy powerful we were together . . . Who would've thought we'd be stronger together?

So much has happened in the last hour, and everything feels different somehow.

After we overcame Audrey at Evie's castle, the truth came out: Ben and I have decided to close the barrier to the Isle of the Lost for good. I'd told Evie and the others that I would bring it down eventually, but I'd lied. Not to be mean, but to protect them. I knew the truth would be painful. How do you explain to your best friend that you're shattering her dreams? That you told her you'd do one thing, but now you have to go back on your word and do the opposite??

EVERY TIME WE OPEN THE BARRIER, SOMETHING bad happens, SOMETHING THAT THREATENS THE SAFETY OF all AURADON CITIZENS. NOW THAT BEN and I ARE RULING THE KINGDOM TOGETHER, WE have TO MAKE THESE IMPOSSIBLE DECISIONS. WE CAN'T KEEP WORRYING about what will happen when one villain comes THROUGH OR BE CONSTANTLY WORRIED about anOTHER villain seeking REVENGE ON a HERO WITHIN THE REALM. WE have TO BE RESPONSIBLE.

Maybe IT DOESN'T MATTER WHAT THE REASONING IS, THOUGH—I Should have JUST TOLD EVIE and UMA THE TRUTH. THEY looked SO HURT and BETRAYED when THEY REALIZED WHAT WAS happening.

Audrey caught us outside the fairy cottage and turned my friends into stone statues. Evie, Carlos, Ben, and Jay—they were all frozen in place, unable to reach me. Evie still had that horrible, disappointed expression on her face, like I'd wronged her in the worst way. I needed help, but Uma and Harry were already gone. They'd been so angry about my lies that they'd abandoned me in the forest. And how could I blame them?? I would've done the same thing.

So when Audrey appeared on Auradon Prep's parapet, holding Celia as her hostage, I was the only one there to fight back. I transformed into a dragon and flew up to face off against her. The problem was my dad's ember had gone out. Without a spark or flame, it has no real power, and Audrey was so much stronger than me. All the energy from the scepter and crown was overtaking me, and I knew I couldn't keep up for long—she was defeating me.

I kept trying to ignite the ember, but no matter how many times I breathed dragon fire onto it, I couldn't get it to spark. Nothing would work.

I started chanting, trying to ignite the ember with a spell, but that didn't work, either. "Regain your might and ignite," I kept saying, knowing it was useless. But then I heard a familiar voice behind me, joining in my chant.
    "Regain your might and ignite." It was Uma. She'd come back to help me—she had my back.

There was nothing better than seeing Uma there, chanting with me, and the ember sparking to life. I don't think I'd ever been so relieved.

AFTER THE EMBER WAS LIT, IT
DIDN'T TAKE LONG FOR US TO OVERPOWER
AUDREY. LIGHT AND ENERGY SHOT OUT
OF THE GLOWING EMBER

AND DRAINED
HER OF HER
STRENGTH.

SHE TRIED TO HOLD ON TO
THE SCEPTER, BUT SHE
WAS GROWING WEAKER
AND WEAKER, AND FINALLY
IT FELL FROM HER HAND.
SHE COLLAPSED ON THE GROUND,
FALLING INTO A DEEP SLEEP.

We didn't know that was going to happen—we couldn't have. But Hades's ember took all the energy from Audrey's sleep spell and turned it back on her, sending her into the deepest slumber.

Everyone knows I don't like princesses, and Audrey was one of the worst of them, but I didn't want this. Mal and I keep wondering and worrying about whether she'll ever wake up.

IT'S SO HARD TO WATCH QUEEN LEAH AND PRINCESS AURORA STAND THERE BESIDE AUDREY'S BED WITH TEARS STREAMING DOWN THEIR CHEEKS. I'VE NEVER SEEN TWO PEOPLE IN SO MUCH PAIN. THEY KEEP STARING AT HER FACE, STUDYING HER LIKE SHE MIGHT SIT UP AND SAY SOMETHING AT ANY MOMENT. THEY KEEP WHISPERING IN HER EAR. AUDREY'S SO STILL, THOUGH . . . EVEN HER EYELIDS HAVEN'T FLICKERED IN SLEEP.

IS SHE GOING TO WAKE UP?? WHEN?? AND IF SHE DOESN'T, ISN'T THIS ALL MY FAULT??

My mother has caused this family so much anguish, and I hate knowing that now I've continued that tradition, even if I didn't mean to. I shouldn't care what Queen Leah thinks of me, but I do. I'm not this vicious villain bent on destroying Audrey's life. I never set out to take her boyfriend or her crown or her kingdom. I didn't want any of this. But then I fell in love with Ben . . . and it all just happened.

I keep saying it, over and over again to myself; please, Audrey . . . please wake up. Come back to us.

Dear Audrey,

I don't know if you'll ever get to read this, but I want you to know that there's still so much I need to say to you. We weren't friends at school, and I know now from what you wrote in your diary that you disliked me. Maybe even more than I disliked you. But still, I hate that this is where we've ended up. I hate that this has happened to both of us.

First off, I never meant to hurt you. That probably doesn't mean much, right?? When I came to Auradon Prep, I was focused on only one thing: getting Fairy Godmother's wand and bringing down the barrier. I didn't care what I did to get the wand. I just knew that I needed it and my mom needed it. Reading what you wrote in your diary, I know now how much pain I caused you. You can't just shrug your shoulders and say the end justifies the means. You can't treat people like stepping stones on your way to some greater goal. This has probably always been so obvious to you, because you were raised to be good, but it's something I had to learn.

Also—I realize now how upset and hurt you were by what happened with Ben, and I'm truly sorry. You have to understand, you're so poised and polished, and you always act like you don't care. I never realized you were so upset about losing him. It always seemed like you were moving on to Chad, or you were just annoyed about not having a chance at being queen anymore. You cared about Ben, and he cared about you. I'm sorry I came between you.

I can't change what happened in the past, but I hope one day things can be different between us. I hope we get that chance.

Mal

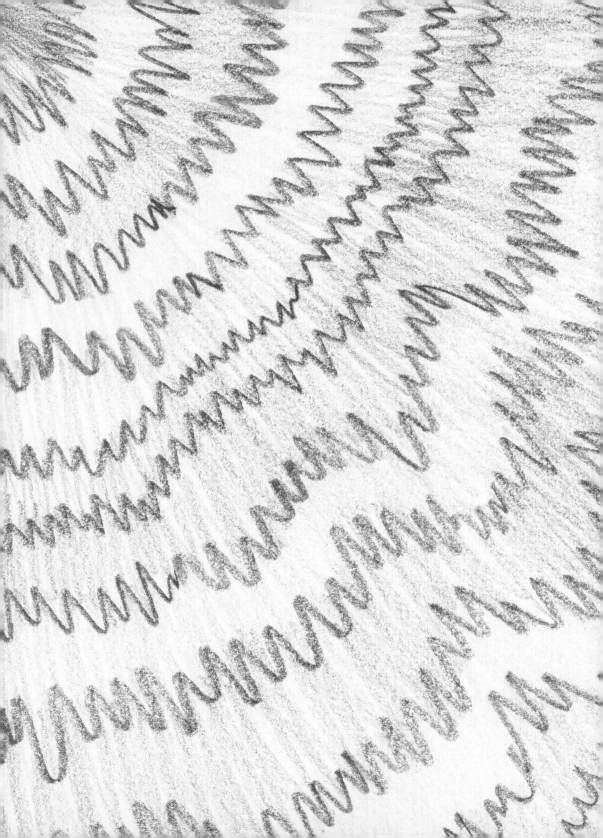

It all seems so faraway, like something that happened in another world. I remember how rageful I was. I can still feel the power from the scepter as it surged through me and gave me strength.

My mom and Grammy told me that Mal and Hades were the ones who finally broke the spell. Mal had Hades brought in from the Isle to help. Since it was Hades's ember that had reversed the sleep spell, turning it back on me, he knew the secret to undoing it. Light and energy swarmed around me, and then I . . . I don't know, I just woke up. I felt like I'd had the most peaceful nap.

It wasn't until I looked at my mother's face that I realized how serious things were. Her eyes were swollen and pink. She must've been crying for days. My grammy was even more upset, because it had all brought up so many horrible memories for her. She was reminded of everything that happened when my mom was a teenager.

That's when I started to remember what I'd done—my part in it. It would be easy to blame Mal, but I had been so vengeful. I just wanted to hurt everyone I could and make everyone pay for all the pain I felt. Mal told me that it wasn't me, that the scepter and crown were controlling me, but I know that at least <u>SOME</u> of it was me. I was the one who decided to steal the crown in the first place. And I went to find the scepter when it called to me in the Auradon museum of Cultural History. I wanted it.

How could I have been so evil?? How could I have done that to all the people I'd grown up with, all the people I'd loved for so long? Even if Ben had wronged me, how could I turn against my kingdom??

I'm so ashamed. . . .

My mom and Grammy had totally different opinions about the engagement party. Grammy said I should stay home and rest, but mom said it would be good for me to get out of the castle. She thought it would be better if I just dove back into the Auradon Prep social scene instead of hiding at the Fairy Cottage with Flora, Fauna, and Merryweather. I mean, Mal and Ben are ruling the kingdom now—at some point I'm going to have to accept that.

I was kind of leaning toward staying home, but then I got an e-mail from Jane. She wanted me to know that she was sorry for making me feel left out. I told her I was sorry for taking her friendship for granted or influencing her to be less than the sweet person she is. I don't know if we're ever going to be best friends, but it made me feel better to know she didn't think I was an evil scepter-charged psycho and she didn't completely hate me for what I'd done to the kingdom. It seemed like proof that Auradon Prep kids were ready to forgive me and move on.

So . . . I went. I WENT TO BEN AND MAL'S ENGAGEMENT PARTY. THEIR ENGAGEMENT <u>PARTY</u>!! Can you <u>believe</u> that?!? I walked in alone, and it took less than three seconds for everyone to welcome me back. People were surrounding me and asking me how I was feeling, and saying they were glad I was back. They were all so nice. I don't think I'll ever be able to hold a grudge again.

I never thought I'd stand in Auradon, looking out over the bay, and cheer for Ben and Mal to bring down the barrier to the Isle of the Lost. But today, at the party, I did just that. Today I clapped and yelled and smiled and was so relieved that it was all over, that the entire kingdom was united and we were all moving on.

I mean, forgiveness is a tricky thing. It took me a while to realize that. I was so angry at Mal for what she'd that it consumed me. But what I did for revenge was so much worse. That sleep spell? It could've destroyed the entire kingdom. Who knows what would've happened if it hadn't been broken, if I hadn't stopped? Turning Ben into a beast? He must've been terrified. And I can only imagine what Mal thought when she saw I'd turned all her friends to stone. She probably thought they were gone forever.

Everyone should've been furious with me. They should've cast me out and said, "That's it. She can never come back to Auradon Prep." But they didn't. Instead, everyone has been kind and understanding. It's breaking my heart a little bit (in a good way).

So if they can forgive me for what I did, I can forgive the villain kids of the Isle of the Lost for all the things they've done in the past. We can start working toward understanding each other and looking for each other's strengths—what unites us instead of what divides us.

At least, I'm going to try to do that from here on out. It feels like it's time.